BATSH*T CRAZY

NATOYA PALMER

Dedication

I want to thank my mother, my deceased father, my two beautiful daughters, my sisters, my nieces, and my nephews. I love you.

Acknowledgements

Thanks to my heavenly father god, my beautiful, rockstar mother Jacqueline, for always supporting me and for reading every page of my book, even when she was tired. Also, thanks to my wonderful daughters, Jhani Kamor, for loving and supporting me no matter what! And memory to my father, Tyrone, the first man to ever love me. And my wonderful aunt Virginia RIP, always in my heart.

Table of Contents

Page Left Blank Intentionally

Chapter One

"Wait till I tell your daddy, Megan! You fucked with the wrong motherfucker's money bitch! Done gave your pa, all my rent money for you, and I didn't even bust a nut."

"It's not my fault you're old and crusty and can't get it up."

Before I knew it, Mr. Smith done tried to hit me. Before I knew it, I had done kicked Mr. Smith in his dick.

I knew before I kicked him, daddy was gonna beat my ass really good. I knew better than to be messing with daddy's money!

Shit is crazy. I have been tricking since I had ass and breasts. Daddy told me when I turned thirteen that I had to take over the family business scene when Momma started smoking crack. Damn shame. I'm seventeen, and daddy still got me tricking and momma still is a crack head. Before I knew it, my dad was flying through the door and punched me in the jaw.

"You long head bitch. What the fuck did you do to Mr. Smith? He's talking about calling the police, so I had to give him that money back. What the fuck did you do bitch? Hurry up and start talking before I fuck you up."

"Mr. Smith couldn't get hard, and he got mad at me. I tried everything to get him hard; nothing would work. He tried to hit me, Daddy, so I kicked him. I was scared, Daddy."

"What you mean that you was scared bitch? My money is fucked up right now because of you. My headlong money is gone, all because of your fast ass. Get dressed bitch, we're about to go find another trick. I want my money back, you long-head bitch."

Before I could get my thoughts together, here comes Momma. "What's your no good? I heard you downstairs talking all fly-in shit to your daddy. You lucky he ain't knocked you the fuck out. All that mouth, girl."

"Momma, Mr. Smith tried to hit me because he couldn't get up. So, I kicked him. I didn't mean to make daddy mad."

"Stop feeling sorry for yourself. Get cleaned up. Ya, daddy already got you a new trick."

"Momma, I can't do this anymore?"

"You can't do what? You think you all that or something? Me and your dad done gave up our whole lives to take care of you. We could have left you at a fucking orphanage. Do you think I wanted this life? I was beautiful before I had you. Beautiful, and chocolate, now you got all my beauty. You know your dad introduced me to Coke? I never sniffed anything in my life. Ya, Dad trapped me with you in drugs. I should have swallowed you and left that dope alone. He knew I was already in love with my drug habit. You know why Mr. Smith couldn't get up for you?"

"Why, Momma?"

"I fucked him an hour before that foul came to your room. Stupid bastard, I wore his ass out. I needed to get high, and your slow-ass dad was taking too long to bring my Coke. So, I fucked him to sleep. I got me some money and some good dope; two for one. Hey, don't tell your dad. You don't get to have all the fun."

As I stood still, looking at my twin mother with tears in my eyes, my door flung loudly open.

"What ya two bitches talking about?"

"Nothing, daddy. I'm so sorry I messed up your money."

"I got some plans for you, girl. I got you a job for three months!"

"What you talking about?"

"The only thing you got to worry about is keeping Mr. Bill King happy while he and his new bride spend their summer vacation without no problems at their family home."

"You mean I got to stay with them for three months? Please, don't send me to stay with strangers. I'll be a good girl, I promise."

"Do you know how much money Mr. King paid me for you? Let

me tell you about life, girl; ain't nothing for free. He done already paid me, and you have an hour to get ready. Megan, give him his money's worth and have a Coke and a smile. Hey girl, don't fuck up my good name. Make me proud. I'm not gonna let you be a loser like your mother turned out to be. Fuck this. Enough of this sensitive shit. You two bitches, are for the birds. Help your daughter get beautiful. Her ride will be here in a while. I can't have her looking like a hot mess."

Chapter Two

"Bill, come get these bad-ass kids of yours! I done cleaned up this house twice already, and I'll be damned if them little bastards will fuck this house up again."

Damn, I hate them kids! I don't understand why Bill didn't put that bitch in her place and tell her that we didn't want the kids for the summer. I wanted to go to Bora Bora for the summer, but instead I'm playing step-mommy to some kids that I don't particularly like. Their momma's gonna come over here, with her old and annoying self, talking about how she's tired and she needs a break.

Me and Bill looked at her like she had two faces, because I knew he just threw her some extra pocket change. Meanwhile, I was waiting for Bill to tell this old, thrifty-looking bitch to go to Hell because we had plans to go to Bora Bora.

Why's Bill gonna lie and tell her that we would love to keep their three kids; gonna lie and say 'my wife's been wanting to spend some quality time. Bill knows good and well that I don't like his kids. I hate when they come over, always crying and touching stuff; always talking about what they don't eat, and always asking if they can ride with us somewhere.

Finally, I just put my foot down and stopped giving him sex for two weeks. I lied and told him the kids coming over all the time was making me less horny and stressing me out. Damn shame we haven't seen them kids in almost a year.

Every time their momma would call, I would make Bill lie and say we had to go out of town or something, or I'd get mad about stupid shit that I knew would piss him off. I know damn well this woman ain't about to come over to my house, just dropping her kids off.

I run Kings Estate, and this ain't no daycare, so she and her kids could go straight to hell. I guess Bill noticed that I was gonna raise Hell like nobody's business. Bill started talking all fast, because he knew that there was gonna be some table-flipping over in this house. Then he had the nerve, in my house, to tell me to go in the other room, so he could talk to her in private. The nerve! So, before I turned my back to walk away, I reminded both of them that they could both kiss my ass.

"What are you screaming for, Kim?"

"Why am I screaming? Because your crazy, bat shit kids, keep messing up this house. I guess you think I'm gonna be the maid and the cook for the summer. You think I married you, so I can play momma to kids that I don't like? You and these kids keep playing with me, and I'm gonna leave you right here, with these bat shit unstable kids, you and your wife brought into the world.”

“I wish you would shut the Hell up for once and have some compassion.”

“Bill, you want me to have compassion for kids that ain’t mine? You made a decision without me to keep kids here without my say so, then you accuse me of not having compassion. Bill, we couldn’t even go on our trip because your ex-wife had beaten you in the face and done threatened you for more money. I knew I shouldn’t let you talk to that mad, selfish bitch without me. Now look what happened. We’re stuck with these kids for the whole summer.”

“What do you want me to do, to make everybody happy?”

“First of all, you could hire a maid and cook, because if you don’t, your kids will be hungry and dirty. Oh, and Bill, don’t think I don’t know about that paid hoe you got coming to stay with us for three months. Oh, cat got your tongue, honey. Don’t get quiet so soon! I want to have fun. You don’t get to have all the fun!”

Chapter Three

"Momma, why do we gotta move from Grandma's house so soon? We just got here two months ago? Where we gonna go? I know you ain't worked in months."

"Hurry up, boy. Momma warned me she didn't want me to be here when she returned home from work. We don't have much time. Momma only gave me thirty minutes to pack my shit up and get out. Mr. Cook is downstairs, ready to take me and your sisters to the bus station."

I was still in shock! I still can't believe I done got caught fucking momma's third husband. Never did I think she would come home early from her day job. That's when Momma caught me and my stepfather making love.

I was so disgusted with myself; I finally broke down and told Momma everything. I told Momma that I was in love with Mr. Cook and my youngest twin daughters, Toya and Tammy, were his. And if I didn't just blow up my life, I also had to confess that my oldest son was my first stepfather's child.

Before I knew it, Momma went to her closet, pulled out a gun and pointed it at me and her husband's head.

"You're about to meet your maker now bitch. Ashley, you done fucked my husband, and I done let you and these bastard kids stay in my home. I should have let you continue getting your ass whooped by that loser you ran away with. I should have known Stud was Kenny's child. As I'm thinking about it, they look like twins! You fucking bitch! You ain't nothing but a scum-bucket whore! Nothing good about you. You're ugly and fat, with no education!"

Even though I was stark naked, I felt the need to defend myself.

"Momma, me and Mr. Cook done fell in love. We had these kids together."

"You stupid fool, he ain't leaving me. He loves money way too much, and I have insurance on his ass. He won't get shit if he leaves me bitch. Get the fuck out of my house whore, before I shoot you both. I'm gonna give you and this fool thirty minutes to get the fuck out of my house. Don't ever contact us again, and if you think for one second my husband will have anything to do with them bastard kids of yours… What his cheating ass will do is drop you at the bus station, because if I ever catch you with my man again, I'm gonna forget you're my child. Now hurry up and get the fuck out!"

Just like that, me and my kids was without a home again. With the little bit of money that I stole from Mr. Cook, while we were making love, I had just enough to get me my three kids' bus tickets, and I also took some bread and baloney. Damn, I fucked up everything. I should have never told Momma about her husbands. Now we were homeless, and I don't have anybody else to blame but me.

Chapter Four

I couldn't wait to get out of that house! Damn, those ugly-ass kids were getting on my last nerves. Always asking me questions, and always crying all the time.

The oldest girl, Amanda, was always asking me questions, like, 'Do I look pretty in this?' I wanted to tell her so bad that she looked just like her mother, hurt in the face, with a fucked-up body.

I had to get out of that house and go to my favorite local dress store. They also had a local Blues club, which I went to on the low. Shit, my husband thinks he can keep secrets, well, I got a few of my own.

Wow, I done spent five-hundred dollars already. Let me get out of this store before I see something else. As I was walking out of the store, I saw this little girl with her hands all over my brand-new Bentley. What the fuck? Don't these kids have manners anymore? Mommas don't teach kids nothing no more. They stand up to grown-ups these days.

"Get your little dirty hands off my Bentley. I should pull off my belt and give you a good beating, girl!"

Wow, I was on a roll. I cussed her out so bad, I didn't realize that this big woman was behind me. Lord, I almost peed on myself when I looked up and saw this angry mother staring at me.

"Why are you cussing at my child like that? If my child touched your car, I'll whoop her tail, but what you will not do is cuss at my child."

I don't know why everybody is fucking with me today. This must be fuck with Ashley day.

"Listen up, woman, I don't give a damn about this car. I'm trying to find the nearest shelter or church. Me and my kids are hungry and tired. I don't got time for your shit, woman. Do you know where the nearest shelter is located?"

"Do you wanna become my maid?"

"What maid? You got me messed up. The last job I had was cooking and cleaning up after Momma and her husband. No, I don't want to become your maid! All I want to do is rest. I'm so tired and sleepy."

"I think you'll like my home better than some nasty shelter. I have a remodeled basement. Just enough room for you and the girls. Just one problem; my husband will have an issue with your grown son staying. Maybe I can find him some work on the estate. Hey, do you want the job, girl? I don't got all day."

"I'll work for you, but I don't want to."

"What's your name, girl?"

"Ashley Booker is my government name. What should we call you?"

"Ashley, you'll address me and my husband as Mr. and Mrs. King. Forgot to ask; do you even cook? What about some cornbread dressing, baked ham, and a little collard greens? Let's go home, Ashley. I'm hungry."

Chapter Five

"Wow, Megan, we done had sex at least four times in a row! Megan, you're one wild little freak! Baby, money well spent. That pussy you got is a ten out of ten. I ain't never felt like this before. I can't wait until Mrs. King drinks some of that pussy. Megan, you got something special between your legs."

"Bill, how much money you pay my dad for me?"

"None of your business, girl. Just concern yourself with making me happy."

Right when I thought Bill was gonna try and go for round five, two women, a young man, and two girls, approached the room that me and Bill shared. My immediate reaction was to cover my face with the covers, but everything happened so quick.

"Oh, Bill, I see why you were trying to rush me out of the house this morning! Your new kept hoe was coming today. Bill, you couldn't wait for me? You're so damn selfish! You sneaky foul, you're gonna have a whole affair in my house, and not let me taste her first? You ain't nothing but a piece of shit, Bill! You sitting there still naked? You ain't even trying to cover yourself."

"This is my house, woman. I do what I please, and wait your turn, my little Megan ain't your bitch to fuck on. So, we have guests?"

"Yes, we do. I found a maid."

"I can see that, but why are these extra kids all up in my house?"

"Our house, remember that. This is Ashley, her son Stud, and her two daughters, Toya and Tara. Ashley has done badly, and she and her kids became homeless."

"We ain't running no homeless shelter, do she even know how to cook? I hope you like other people's kids, because watching my children comes with the job. I'm a very busy man and my children are annoying little buggers, so make sure you keep them busy and away from me."

"Ashley, excuse my husband's bedside manner, he's done got him a new piece of ass, and don't know how to act."

"Don't speak for me, woman! We have an unusual household around here. Just to let all y'all know, I'm the king of this castle, and if anybody got a problem with what I said, you can get the fuck out!"

Chapter Six

"Ashley, round everybody up; we are about to have a family picnic. Make sure you include Megan. Make sure my step-kids look decent, and remind them that if they don't like me, I don't like their asses either. Ugly ass little girl. She's just mad her daddy loves me and I ain't going nowhere. Ashley, I'm gonna end up putting my hands on that little heifer."

"Kim, you something else. I'll make sure everybody is on their best behavior. Kim, this picnic will be me and my kids' and my first picnic ever. Stud, Megan, what the fuck are y'all doing? We just dancing and having a little fun, Megan, me, and my children got something good around here. Don't put your voodoo on my son! Do I make myself clear? Didn't mean to cause a problem, Ashley. We just heard this new blues song, and before we knew it, we just started dancing. Listen, Megan, I'm not gonna go back and forth with you. If I got to talk to you again, it's gonna be hand and feet, you get me, girl. Can't stand you, pretty bitches, always acting like everybody is crazy.

Anyway, I need y'all's help. Mrs. King invited everybody to a picnic, and I need help setting up the food outside. Shit, can't believe

I'm having so much fun. I was so mad a while ago, all I wanted to do was to dot Ashley's eye. I wanted to actually see if her butt could really fight. Next time, Ashley, come for me, I'm going zero to a hundred. I'm definitely with that shit! I should have had a picnic for the kids years ago. All I wanted was to sit around being lazy. We never did anything fun. My fun time was when Momma went to work. Me and my mother's husband would pretend like we were a big happy family. That was my idea of fun. My picnic was a wonderful idea.

Everybody seems to be enjoying themselves, even my stepkids. Couldn't help but glance at Stud. He sure is fine!

Chapter Seven

"You two bitches get up!"

"Kim, it's five o'clock in the morning, my shift won't start until seven."

"Ashley, I want you and Megan to meet me at the family pond." "The pond? I don't swim, Kim. I just roller set my hair."

"I know I don't have no swimsuit. I'm sure Ashley don't own a swimsuit either."

"Ashley, I'm from Paris, we don't swim with bathing suits, we going skinny dipping. Come on, girl, I'll meet you and Megan at the family pond in twenty minutes."

"Come on bitches jump in."

"Kim, I don't know about Ashley, but I don't know how to swim."

"Listen bitches, if y'all gonna hang with me, y'all gonna have to loosen the fuck up. And while we're not working, I would like you'll to call me Kim. This is your bitches lucky day. I'm gonna teach y'all how to swim."

While we were returning from our swim, I noticed my in-laws' Cadillac parked in the driveway. Fuck, I forgot they were coming today. Can't stand them bitches. Always looking down on me, like their shit don't stank! Breakfast was the longest shit ever. My mother-in-law never minced words.

"So, I see my granddaughter and two grandsons will be staying for the summer? If I hear about your nothing ass being mean to my grandkids, there'll be hell to pay. Do you understand? Do I make myself clear? It's not their fault you can't have children. Me and my Eric should have done a background check on you. Now we're stuck with you."

I couldn't believe I was listening to Bill's mother cuss Kim all the way out, and she was just taking it. Before I knew it, Bill done come behind me, slid my dress up, and literally put his whole hand in between my legs. As he stroked me a few times, I came immediately. All I could think about was how turned on I was.

"Ashley, my mother would like some more eggs. Ashley, be a doll and make me some pancakes, you done got me hungry girl!"

Chapter Eight

"Amanda, why you never tell anybody that you wanted me to become a women's doctor?"

"Thanks for checking on my box, I've done let your grandfather nut all up inside. You know he's up in age, and he could have given me worms."

"Megan, you so funny. Your vagina looks perfect. Just let me know when your period arrives, okay?"

"Thanks, Amanda, I never knew you were so cool." "Megan, how does it feel when a boy likes you?"

"You'll know, because he won't leave you alone. Just in case he does go missing, never look back and go on to the next. Men are just like tools. Use them like they use you."

"So, you and Kim getting along any better?"

"No, she doesn't like me or my little brothers, and we don't like her dusty self either."

"Amanda, your stepmother has been hurt in the past. Hurt people usually hurt the person that they're closest to. Don't ask me why, they just do."

"Bill, your parents are still here! It's been weeks and they ain't left yet. They're driving me crazy."

"I forgot to share with you. Dad got the nerve and told me he's turning the estate that we live in, and turning my land into three different sections. He wants to build a summer resort and a farm, and he wants to build two-bedroom cottages for the employees. Dad got me fucked up; he also wants me to help with the project."

"Pass me that joint, Kim? I'm stressed the fuck out. I'm getting too old to be working in the field. My dad is a crazy old bastard. I even offered him my baby, Megan, to help change his mind. All he did was give me a check to double the price I spent on Megan. He's got the balls to tell me I can never touch my own bitch again. Can you believe it, Kim? I'm banned from my own bitch! Gonna call me lazy, I got right back with him and said I'm a lazy motherfucker and I'm alright with that."

Chapter Nine

"Ashley, Megan, I'm hearing way too much about this new club they built downtown called The Hotel. It's a new jazz and blues club. Tonight, we will be going."

"Kim, we ain't going anywhere with you. You can't even dance.

You don't have no rhythm, not even a little bit. Kim, you're not gonna embarrass me. Let me and Megan teach you a few dance moves."

"Girls, I don't have to know how to dance. All I have to do is show a little bit of money, and my night will be lit. Meet me downstairs around eight o'clock. I have to have a mandatory dinner with my mother-in-law and stepkids."

"Pass the potato salad, Amanda."

"Kim, is there anything wrong with your reach. Kim, the potato salad is right by you, and you want me to get it for you? If you say please, I just might think about it."

"You done slid down a razor blade and landed in an alcohol river, girl. What's got you handling me that way? Slow your roll before I forget you're Bill's child."

"Watch how you talk to my granddaughter, Kim! You're about to make me turn this whole table on top of your head. Kim, keep coming for my grandchild, and you're gonna find what you're looking for!"

"You want my stepdaughter to disrespect me, Jackie?"

"Kim, fuck you as a person. I never liked you and never will. I warned Bill you would trap him. You can't even carry kids due to that nasty women's disease you had before you met my son. Kim, you thought I wasn't gonna find out about your past. Bill snuck and married you. You know me and my grandkids have to sit with your nothing ass! My son done married a god damn roach!"

Before I knew it, I grabbed two helpings of Ashley's famous potato salad and threw it directly in their face.

"You're gonna respect me, old lady, and Amanda, we're shipping your grown ugly ass off to boarding school. I never wanted either of you to come to my house!"

"As if I give a damn."

Amanda yelled out, "Stay away from Stud! I saw you flirting with him."

"Stud is almost a grown man; he would never want you."

Bill's mother flat-out called me a cheating whore. Before I could fix my mouth to talk some more shit. My mother-in-law done turned the whole table over on me. All the food that was on the table fell right on top of me. I was covered with food. And if that wasn't enough, Bill's mother and Amanda started punching me in the head.

I immediately fell to the ground and covered my face. All I knew was that I could feel someone kick me in the head. Couldn't believe one of these bitches just kicked me. They were screaming at me, saying how much they hated me. It seemed like the beat down was for hours.

Bill must have heard all the commotion and ran into the house.

He pulled his mother and daughter off my face. As if his mother wasn't done with me, her old senior citizen ass done back-handed me.

She said, "This is my house and don't you forget it, you little cunt."

They done finally beat my ass! I looked and felt like I just got jumped by an angry group of men, not women.

Chapter Ten

As weeks went by, old wounds healed, new relationships bloomed, and the new expansion on Mr. King's resort was starting to become the talk of the town. Gossip was that Mr. King was to make billions of dollars off his new resort project.

"Mrs. King, I told you we had to stop messing around! Mr. King will kill me if he finds out about our affair. Stop, your husband is down the road. What if he walks in?"

Wow, the thought of that made me laugh just a little bit. Bill was walking in, while Stud's twelve-inch penis was sliding in and out of my mouth. My mouth had never felt this kind of penetration, ever. Shit, Stud made sure my tonsils were massaged every night.

"Bill and his father are busy working on the resort project. Bill ain't thinking about me. Bill's probably fucking Megan as we speak. Don't worry, Stud, he will never find out. Stud, didn't I tell you when the resort is finished, I'm gonna make Mr. Bill make you head manager of the resort. You're gonna have your own money, and y'all never have to worry about asking a soul for money ever."

As if money was the magic word, Stud done turned me around, as if he didn't want to look me in the face, and started pounding the shit out of my asshole.

"Eric, is this horse really for me?"

"Yes, ain't she a beauty? Megan, this horse is a Thorough Fusaichi Pegasus. Only the best for my Megan."

"Eric, you have to stop buying me all these expensive gifts. You just purchased me a ten-carat diamond necklace. Your Jackie's gonna find out about us soon. I don't want your wife, Jackie, to put a whooping on me, like she gave to your daughter-in-law."

"Don't worry about my wife. She already knows about us. I'm the head of this household. I give out all the orders, but I don't receive them."

"What am I gonna do with a horse?"

"I'm going to be leaving to go home soon, Megan. I forgot to tell you. I paid your trifling father a visit a few days ago. I paid him a nice, generous amount of money to never contact you ever again. So, for now, this is your home, until I build you your own home on your own land. How does that sound, my sweet Megan?"

"Nobody has ever treated me so good."

"The way you make me feel, Megan, you're gonna be financially set for the rest of your life."

"Ashley, you better be making me that homemade beef stew like I asked you for yesterday."

"Bill, why are you in this kitchen messing with me for? Bill, don't you see all the ingredients laid out on the counter?"

"Ashley, you're my kind of girl. Fuck me and feed me, that's why I fuck with you. Ashley, you're the best cook I've ever had, and that way you ate my asshole out last night… Ashley, you got serious skills."

Before I could give Bill a kiss, I heard my daughter, Toya, screaming from outside. I ran outside to find Bill's wild hen pecking my daughter's face. Good thing Toya had really thick glasses on, because that hen was aiming for her eye. Within seconds, I heard a loud gunshot. Bill done shot the hen right in the head. Bill saved my daughter's life. Not only was I falling for Bill, but I owed him for saving my sweet daughter's life. My kids were my lifeline.

Chapter Eleven

"Ashley, Megan, guess who's performing tonight at The Hotel? Tony Long and the Peanuts. They're about to show up and show out! Don't worry about clothes, I already picked out your clothes. You bitches won't be embarrassing me."

"I hope you practiced those dance moves we taught you. We don't want you to embarrass us."

"Kim, get in here; come look at this piece of shit letter!"

"Why are you yelling so loudly? The whole house can hear you?"

"This bitch done lost her mind. I should have never let her trifling ass talk me into keeping these kids."

"What's going on, Bill?"

"The kids' mother just wrote us this 'dear John' letter and announced that she's never coming back for the children. The letter also says to tell my children that she loves them."

"That stinking ass bitch. I should have let you dot her damn eye that day. I knew she was gonna try some shit. We should have never let her, or them crazy-looking kids, in the house. Anyways, your kids, your problem!"

Honestly, I really don't give three fucks about Bill's kids. The only thing on my mind right now is Tony Long, a drink, and a hook-up. We danced so much our legs caught a cramp.

One thing about Megan and Ashley is that they truly were a whole bunch of fun. All of us were secretly starting to adore each other.

"Okay, Megan, shake that money maker!"

"Girl, hurry up and get the fuck out of here. You really be tripping! If anyone catches you in here, I'm a dead man."

"Nobody's gonna find out about you and me."

"Ain't no you and me!"

"Stud, baby, I need you."

"My mother done abandoned me and my little brothers; just left us with these bat-shit crazy people."

"I'm telling you right now that tonight will be our last night together. You're lucky that pussy is good!"

Chapter Twelve

"Ashley, what was in that breakfast you cooked? Something got my stomach so fucked up. I threw up at least three times already! I never get sick."

"Kim, you probably caught a stomach bug."

"Ashley, this pain feels like something different. I'm really sick to my stomach."

"Kim, I'll call y'all family doctor on your behalf and see if he can come by."

"Ashley, what if this is something serious?"

"Kim, ain't nothing wrong with you; just the stomach bug that's all."

While waiting for the doctor to come treat. Kim, I noticed that Megan, Amanda, and eventually, with all the sickness going around, I started to become nauseous. With ten seconds, I started to throw up all over the floor. I was so overwhelmed with dizziness and nausea that I fell flat on my face. While waking up from my sudden drop to the floor, I was so confused to find all of us sick and in the same room. Kim must have requested us to be roomed together due to the mysterious stomach bug going around the house.

Kim was the first one to ask the doctor, "Will we all be okay?"

"Doc, is this the stomach bug, or did we eat something rotten?"

"It's neither, ladies. Congratulations, you're pregnant!"

"Kim, Bill will be so excited. I was starting to believe you couldn't carry children."

My worry was Bill's young daughter, Amanda. I didn't know she was old enough to be courting or having sex. I knew Bill would be furious when he found out.

"Please don't inform Bill. I would like to tell him about my good news first, then mention him becoming a grandfather."

"I'll let you ladies rest. Pregnancy can sometimes drain all the energy from a woman's body. Just old-fashioned morning sickness. Mrs. King, Amanda, Ashley, and Megan, I promise that in a couple of weeks, the morning sickness will disappear."

All I could think about was Bill's hands around my throat. Damn, this baby couldn't possibly be Bill's child. We stopped having sex months ago.

"These sneaky-ass bitches, who the hell knocked their asses up?"

Damn, this is some karma for real. We are all pregnant!

Chapter Thirteen

I must have lost my fucking mind letting this old man fuck on me, he should have been pulling out. I never had a mother or father who loved me. I don't know if I even love myself.

Fuck, I remember when Eric nutted inside me. My ass was so happy about the diamond necklace he purchased for me. I must have gotten beside myself and thought I was a better bitch or something.

Damn, I should have swallowed. I knew this good pussy was too much for his old ass. Can't believe I'm knocked the fuck up and sick as hell.

"Megan, are you pregnant by my bird-ass husband?"

"Kim, I haven't fucked Bill in a while! Bill pulls out every time. Eric's been nutting inside me on the regular, and done trapped me. Eric's wife is probably gonna see if I can fight. Kim, I'm gonna have to brawl with a senior citizen."

"Yeah, she does have a mean lift hook! That's how she punched me in the eye. My mother-in-law had my eye on ice for almost a week. So, who you got the nerve to be pregnant by Amanda? Bill's gonna tear your ass up when he finds out. Wow, I thought you was a virgin in your around here fucking. Look at the fleas on fluffy, somebody done got your ugly ass pregnant."

"Kim, I'm so nauseous I refuse to go back and forth with the likes of you."

"Ms. Ashley, me and your son are in love; we've been messing around for a while now."

"You fuckin' cunt. I'm pregnant with Stud. Fuck you, Kim. My grandmother and mother always said you were a cum-sucking back-alley way ass bitch from Paris. You've been cheating on my father, and now you're caught, you crusty bitch."

"Do you wanna fight Amanda? Granny ain't here to help you. I'm gonna put my foot right in your ass."

Before I could reach out and touch that bitch, Ashley had mustered up some strength to pull us apart.

"I'm not gonna let y'all fight. If you're both pregnant by my dumb-ass son, that makes me the grandmother of your unborn babies. Damn, my son is a dead man walking. Stud done impregnated the stepmother and the daughter. He really done lost his mind. I can't keep quiet about my sins. Kim, I'm pregnant with your husband. Bill and I been fucking on the low for a while now. I knew I should've kept my pussy to myself. Kim, I'm your husband's whore, and he's in love with all of this pussy. Even though I feel like a piece of shit, we're family now, and y'all stuck with me and Stud.

Chapter Fourteen

"Clean up women. Calm down. You're not relevant or important. You've been hooking up with married men! I knew who you were the second day you moved into my home. Bill's ass didn't trust you since day one, so he hired a private detective to do a background check on you. Ashley, you ain't nothing but your stepfather's whore. Say it ain't so. I can tell by your bitch-ass eyes. Oh, and don't let this go over your head, Ashley, he doesn't fuck with the kids he already has. Don't sit there and think that you are special."

"Kim, I never meant to hurt you."

"Hurt me, Ashley? You could never, but I do think that you're fucking with me, though. Save them fake-ass tears for someone else, you raggedy bitch. I got your dimes and nickels, Ashley."

"I wish you in. Kim would stop yelling. I'm truly sick. I think something is wrong with the baby."

"I'll call the doctor again; he maybe can make another house visit."

"Ashley, inform your son that he fucked up the church's money by getting the stepmother and the daughter pregnant. He's so finished when Jackie finds out about the pregnancies. Bill's mother is a bitch on wheels. Jackie has been waiting for me to fuck up. We are all fucking finished. Stud, get your two-timing ass up. You've been sticking your dick inside Kim and Amanda, and now we finished. Stud, you've impregnated both of them."

"Stud, it's 1957, and I'm not trying to have my only son shot for fucking a rich whore. Did you forget that Mrs. Kim and Amanda are wealthy, and you ain't got a pot to piss in and a window to throw it out of."

"If anything, Ma, them bitches took advantage of me."

Before I could dot my son in the eye, Mrs. Jackie's personal maid just walked in the room and said, "Mrs. King will need everybody downstairs for a meeting."

Damn, she really is a bitch on wheels!

Chapter Fifteen

Damn, I just knew shit was about to go down when I saw Ashley, Stud, and Amanda walking into the living room with the slow bop. Every last one of us had this 'we got caught' guilty look on our faces. Bill's ass came walking in ten minutes later like he was King Tut. He had the nerve to ask why he didn't smell his food cooking.

"Where is my food? I came home early, because I thought the letter that my mom and father had delivered to me was informing me of a dinner party or something. Can someone inform me why y'all look like someone shot your dog?"

Before I could confess to Bill and inform him about all the whoring around I'd done behind his back, Jackie and Eric appeared quietly in the living room. Jackie had her Sunday best on, with that stank-ass perfume that she loved to wear. Eric had this dumb smile on his face, as if he had won a damn prize or something. I instantly got irritated and nauseous.

"I hate to be rude, Jackie and Eric, but I have better things to do today. I have the stomach bug and my mood ain't good today."

"Oh, the same stomach bug Megan has? The nine-month stomach bug? You lying bitch. Listen, me and my husband are gonna keep this conversation short and sweet. Megan has extreme morning sickness; the doctor called it hyperemesis, and he also believes she has a blood clot in her arm.”

“Sounds horrible, but what does Megan’s sickness got anything to do with y’all interrupting my day. I’m sick too. Y’all gonna throw me a pity party?”

“Bill, you better get your bitch. Jackie, aren’t you mad? Eric?”

Eric was still throwing his big dick around, impregnating bitches.

“Why are you in Eric and Megan’s business? You must be bored or something. You don’t have a card party to go to or something?”

“Megan is pregnant with my husband's child, which makes Megan our family and the business of mine. Bill, you and that hot box of a wife you have, got to get the fuck up out of my home. And, please take your extended family with you.”

“Where do you expect us to live, Mother?”

“I’m really not concerned where you’re going. But, your father done taken pity on you and your new extended family. Your father is loaning you the three-bedroom cottage.”

“The fucking cottage by the barn? What is everybody gonna think when they find out you kicked us out? Mom, you got some nerve thinking that me and my whole family are supposed to stay in a three-bedroom cottage near some fucking wildlife animals, and by the main barn."

"Stop your whining, boy, and please go quietly. Megan is experiencing extreme morning sickness, and we need peace and quietness. Bill, don't even pack or move anything. My personal movers are packing y'all's shit as we speak."

"Damn, Jackie, you really are a cold-ass woman. Jackie, you gonna kick two pregnant women out, and his two young boys. Jackie, you always thought you were a better bitch. You bleed once a month just like me."

"Fall in line, Kim, before you become financially fucked up! Now, get the fuck out!"

Chapter Sixteen

Can't believe I've been living in this three-bedroom shack for nine months. Nasty-ass Jackie has us living in a mere one-acre, three-bedroom, piece-of-shit cottage. While I'm living life in this fucking hovel, Eric and Jackie are living in my massive mansion, which was promised to me and Bill. They really got us out here looking poor and thrifty!

"Damn, and here you go creeping beside me looking dumb, got me about to get nauseous. Knock on the bedroom door first, don't just come busting up in here, all in my face, smelling like Ashley. Bill, you smell like musk, garlic, and Ashley's cheap perfume! Stank ass!"

"Don't worry about my stench, you miserable bitch. You dirty cunt whore, got the nerve to be upset? Kim, you're just mad because you got caught fucking our maid's broke son. Kim, you truly are a dumb bitch. At least you could have gotten pregnant by someone with money. Your unborn baby is by a young, broke punk that I employ. Which way did your mind go bitch? You really think I'm about to fund your bastard baby, but you got me fucked up. As soon as you drop that load, you're getting the fuck out of my house!"

"Oh, don't you mean your parents' house. Whatever, Bill, this ain't no house. This is a motherfucking hole in the wall; a fucking hovel. Bill, don't forget we're still married and I ain't going nowhere. Remember, Bill, till death do us part. Did you forget that you got Ashley pregnant, and your slut daughter is walking around here pregnant too?"

"Don't you fret bitch, as soon as these unplanned burdens are born, all y'all cunts are getting out. You never really had shit before I met you. I took care of you, Kim. I gave you life. Kim, you ain't no different from one of them begging-ass bums on the street. Tired ass hoe. Kim, I only came upstairs to tell you that my private detective found Amanda's mother. Oh, and my parents are having a huge dinner party Saturday to celebrate the grand opening of the King's resort. So, make sure you put your Sunday best on, and don't forget to fake smile."

"Oh, they found your track-star kid's mother?"

"Yeah, they found her nerdy ass living in Jamaica. She really was out there, living her best life off my money. Amanda's goofy, bird-brained mother really got me fucked up, if she thought I was gonna take care of Amanda and her bastard child. Amanda's mother is gonna respond back, talking about giving her an extra thousand dollars a month to take in Amanda's baby."

"You'd better give her that money, Bill. You know I can't stand looking at Amanda, with her bad body. Pregnancy really looks awful on Amanda. I'm really ready for her to get the fuck out."

"Kim, you getting out too, don't forget."

"Bill, you're talking out of the side of your neck. I'm not going anywhere. I'm gonna stay right here and live off the land, and make you and your parents miserable. Bill, fuck you, your hillbilly parents, their party, and tell them I ain't coming, and they can suck my dead dog's dick!"

"Why the fuck are you at my doorstep, woman? I hope you ain't selling shit because I'm broker than a motherfucker."

"I'm here to see Jason Smith."

"What do you want from me, woman?" "My name is Jackie King."

"Oh, you came to drop my pregnant daughter off? Your rotten husband gets Megan pregnant, and you're here to drop her off with me?"

"Of course not. I came all the way here to tell you to stop blackmailing Eric King. Jason, you send one more letter, or show up at my home again, and I'll put your ass right in the ground."

"Eric better be paying me some more money. Y'all really think that I would stay away from my daughter and grandchild? Mrs.

Jackie, you're really getting on my nerves with your rich, funky ass. Listen up, young mute. My husband paid you a few dollars already, and I'm not paying you shit. If I hear about you trying to blackmail my beautiful husband again, I will personally get rid of you.

Jason, you don't want me as your enemy! My name is Jackie, I'm the fucking bone collector. You don't want these problems; I'll fuck your whole life up."

Chapter Seventeen

"Mrs. Jackie, I'm not eating any more liver or beans."

"Megan, hush, liver has a lot of protein."

"Jackie, I just want a little bit of junk food."

"Ever since I hired the nutritionist, you haven't been sick. That's because you have been eating right."

"Well, you are right about me not getting as sick lately. Mrs. Jackie, how could you stand looking at me while I'm pregnant by Eric?"

"Megan, all your life, men used you for their own selfish game. I'm truly sorry for my son and my husband. I promise you that I will always take care of you and the baby. Don't you wanna finish school?"

"I would love to go back to school. I can't any more, because the baby is about to come."

"Megan, if you wanna go back to school, or even go to school out of state, I'll support you. Megan, your baby is a King. Your child is already a billionaire. I just want you to know that you have options."

"Jackie, since I'm feeling well, I really wanna meet Ashley and the kids at the pond. We haven't seen each other in months."

"Megan, just please be careful. Don't be at that pond fooling around. Accidents happen every day."

"I'll be okay. I just need some fresh air. I do want to go back to school, with kids my own age, I can relate to."

"Whatever you wanna do in life, Megan, I'll support you." While I was approaching the pond, I saw Kim.

"I'm on my way to the pond. You coming to chill?" "Is Ashley snake ass gonna be there?"

"She should be already there. Girl, I know damn well you ain't still mad at Ashley."

"I'm still mad at that cum-sucking bitch. That bum bitch can kick rocks."

"Kim, shut your mad pregnant ass up and let's go skinny dipping."

"Ashley, you and Kim better not interrupt my time in this pond or I will drown both you bitches."

"Can't believe this man got y'all acting like a bunch of birds " "Whatever, Megan, I ain't worried about this bitch no more.

Soon, we will be leaving for good."

"Why?"

"My mother is in the hospital. She's really sick. I'm going to take care of her, and plead with her, to forgive me for all my whorish ways."

"Bitch, what about Bill? You gonna just leave your baby daddy?"

"Girl, fuck him. Kim, his stank ass has been cheating on both of us anyway. I found a hickey on his dick. Cheating bastard got me fucked up. Girl, I want to do his ass real dirty and leave this baby right with his cheating ass. Just thinking about having another child that I'm gonna have to take care of by myself has got me bitter as hell. I'm on that each one teach one type of time, I'm already planning my escape. I'm planning on running away with Tony Long."

"Kim, you still fucking Tony?"

"Hell yeah. Men love pregnant pussy. I never stopped fucking him. I've been getting that dick. I also fucked his background singer, Peanut."

"Kim, you ain't shit. Kim, you talked about me so bad, but you out here cheating on your husband and my son."

"Ashley, fuck you, you bothered-ass bitch. I'm gonna hit both of y'all with my 'nigga be cool' bat if y'all start arguing again. Ashley, are you gonna be cooking for the dinner party tonight?"

"I told Jackie that I'll help. I hope you make some chitlins, dressing, potato salad, corn bread, and greens. I've been craving that shit. Jackie got me eating some type of protein food with no seasonings allowed."

"Kim, you going to the dinner party tonight?"

"I wasn't planning on going. I really don't like looking at that old raggedy bitch."

"You might want to attend, because Bill's kid's mother is supposed to be there and she's coming to take her kids with her."

"I knew about that. Amanda already informed Stud. I'm kinda glad she's leaving. I don't want to be nobody's grandmother. Shit, I don't even want this baby."

"Whatever bitch. You should have swallowed it. Anyway, Kim, are you coming to the dinner party tonight?"

"I think I might attend so I can inform Amanda's mother about all the hell her kids done raised."

Chapter Eighteen

"Megan, I can't believe Jackie invited that runaway baby-mother to a family dinner?"

"Both of them are simple bitches who are dumb. Megan, that country bird done abandoned her kids for months, and she gets to come to a family function. While I've been here playing mother hen to her bad-ass kids. Not to mention Amanda stank bad body ass done fucked Stud. Jackie better hurry up and get them bitches up out of here!"

"Well, everyone is downstairs, so please don't go downstairs and embarrass yourself. Megan says less, all of them phony bitches can be great. Amanda and her slack mother better hurry up and make moves, before I dot both of them in the eye."

I know I told Megan that I wasn't gonna act up, but as soon as I saw Amanda's mother, I stepped up to her.

"Look at the fleas on fluffy! Your mute ass, just gonna bring yourself in this house, like you didn't just abandon your kids."

Before she had a chance to open her mouth, to say some slick shit, I done knocked her thick glasses straight off her face. I know her face was on fire because I totally forgot I had my rings on.

Jackie started screaming at me, talking about how I better get my wild nothing-ass out of her home. Jackie had the nerve to grab my whole arm and twist it to the back!

Amanda's pregnant ass ran up on me and sucker punched me in the head, while Jackie still had my arm twisted to the back. Ashley and Megan came out of nowhere and grabbed a handful of Amanda's hair and swung her to the floor.

When Jackie saw Megan fighting, that's when she wanted everybody to stop brawling.

"Fuck that, Jackie, I'm not gonna let y'all jump on just one person."

Just when I thought I was about to fuck a bitch up, I felt the worst pain in my stomach I've ever felt. As though it was a domino effect, we all started screaming in pain, one by one, our water broke at the same time.

Jackie started ordering everybody around, yelling at the maids to grab hot towels, sheets, and blankets. Kim had the nerve to still be talking shit, gonna tell Jackie that she could kiss her dirty pillows.

Kim started yelling as loud as she could, talking about not trying to handle her, and that she didn't want Jackie's old, decrepit ass delivering her baby.

"Don't try to hustle me, Jackie. I have options for the best doctors in New York State. Call my doctor, you old bitch."

"Kim, you're gonna learn today that I'm the head-bitch in charge. So, shut the fuck up, and let your baby come properly into the world."

Ashley's baby boy came first, weighing eight pounds. Kim and Amanda's baby boys weighed eight pounds, and my little baby girl came in weighing four pounds. Say what you want about Jackie, she delivered all four babies by herself and didn't even break a sweat.

Chapter Nineteen

"Megan, I don't mean no harm or no disrespect, but it's time for me to kick rocks."

"What's your crazy self, talking about Kim?"

"I'm about to kick myself out of this house. Tony Long is expecting me to meet up! I'm going on the road with him. That sounds so selfish, Kim. You just gonna leave your sweet baby boy for a man?"

"Girl, bye. Me and big dick Tony got plans. Megan, I'm gonna moon walk up out of here, too."

"Ashley, your dumb ass about to walk out on your baby, too?"
"Fuck you, Megan. I will not be left taking care of another child by myself. Where is Amanda?"

"Amanda and her mother got up out of here as soon as the doctor checked her pussy. Amanda's mother is getting an extra thousand dollars to help raise the baby."

"That bitch left before my son could even see his son. I only got a chance to peek at my first grandson. Amanda did some sucker shit because we knocked her funky ass to the ground. Come on, Kim, before Jackie's old ass comes in here and starts getting in our business."

"Jackie better not ask me where I'm going.

"Who's going to take care of your boy that y'all about to abandon?"

"Jackie's old, crusty, wrinkled face ass is gonna take care of our sons. It's only karma for her son treating me so badly through the years."

"Meghan, soon, you're gonna be the only one in this miserable house. Make sure you tell our boys that we love them!"

Jackie came walking into the room an hour later, with this smug look on her face.

"Megan, I saw those rats sneaking out, looking like a hot mess. Straight out of their delivery bed, they'll probably bleed all the way to the train station. Them bitches are probably gonna catch an infection up the ass. Weird ass cunts. I'm not surprised that the hoes ran off. They thought their dimes and nickels were slick when they found out that Bill was disinherited and your daughter would inherit everything.

"Kim and Ashley ran off, because they knew that I would love and protect them babies with all my soul. God is on their side, because, if I were to ever run into either one of them whores, it would be me and them, and mostly me. I remember when Bill brought that trash into my home. I truly tried to like her at first, but the bitch got beside herself. Kim definitely started smelling herself. That musty cunt bitch.

"Kim would have been the perfect wife, until she found out me and Eric still owned everything, and she went bat shit crazy, and now she done left me with her child. I also did a background check on her and found out that she was a whore from Paris, France. Kim got my son to feel sorry for her, and he married her without a prenup. Bill had lost his mind. I didn't mind disinheriting his dumb ass. Ain't no bitch without a soul will ever get any money from the Kings."

"Jackie, you never gave them a chance."

"Megan, them bitches got me fucked up. They were so thirsty to abandon their own babies that they didn't even wash their asses.

Both of them have stitches all up the asshole. I also did a background check on Ashley, and don't you know that she purposely seduced all of her mother's husbands. Ashley's nasty self even got kids by her own stepfathers. Not to mention her sperm donor son, done got Amanda and Kim pregnant. Stud had been throwing around his penis in every scene he got here.

"Megan, as you can tell about me, I don't like for anyone to treat my grandkids fucked up. Kim's lucky I didn't dislocate her arm the other day. Megan, I really want you to have a good life. Eric and me, if you want, will send you to the college of your choice, all expenses paid for. Megan, if you're not interested in school at this time, you will always be welcome to live on our land forever.

Megan, get some sleep, babies love to wake up when their parents are tired."

"Thanks, Jackie, I'll take you up on that offer to go to college!" "Megan, I can see you as a college grad."

THE END